塞翁失馬

近塞上之人。有善術者。馬無故亡而入胡。人皆弔之。其父曰。此何遽不為福乎。居數月。其馬將胡駿馬而歸。人皆賀之。其父曰。此何遽不能為禍乎。家富良馬。其子好騎。墮而折其髀。人皆弔之。其父曰。此何遽不為福乎。居一年。胡人大入塞。丁壯者引弦而戰。近塞之人。死者十九。此獨以跛之故。父子相保。

《淮南子·人間訓》

THE LOST HORSE

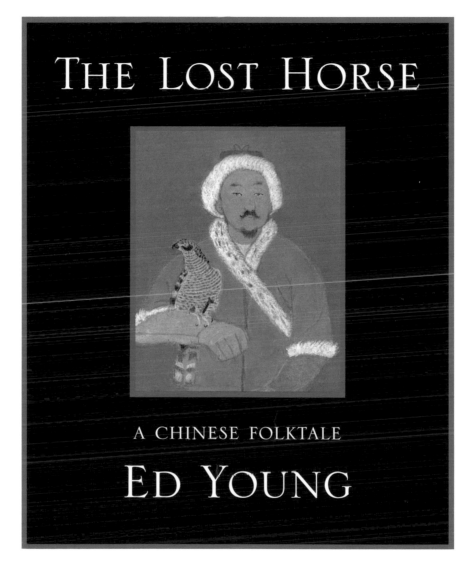

A CHINESE FOLKTALE

ED YOUNG

Silver Whistle

Harcourt Brace & Company

SAN DIEGO   NEW YORK   LONDON

PRINTED IN SINGAPORE

IN NORTHERN CHINA there once lived a wise man called Sai.

He had few possessions but owned
a horse that was both strong and fast.

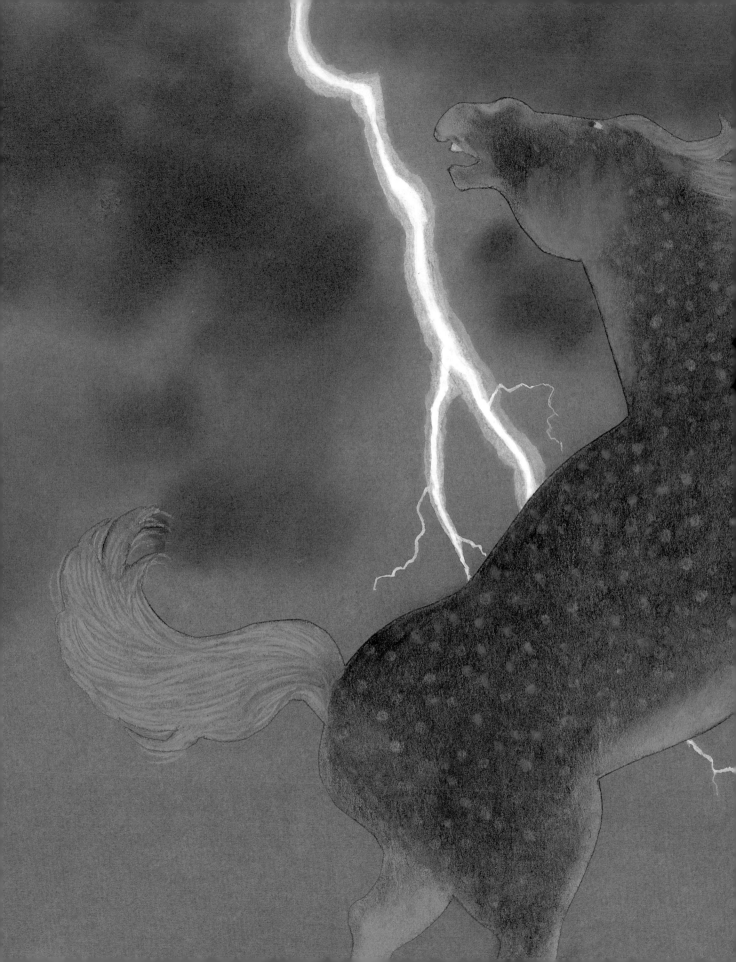

One day a violent thunderstorm struck the land.
Terrified, the horse escaped into the night.

One by one the people came to comfort Sai for his loss.
"You know, it may not be such a bad thing,"
he told them.

To the people's surprise, the horse returned a few
days later with a mare, equally fast and strong.

When the people came to congratulate Sai on his good fortune, he replied, "Perhaps it is not such a good thing."

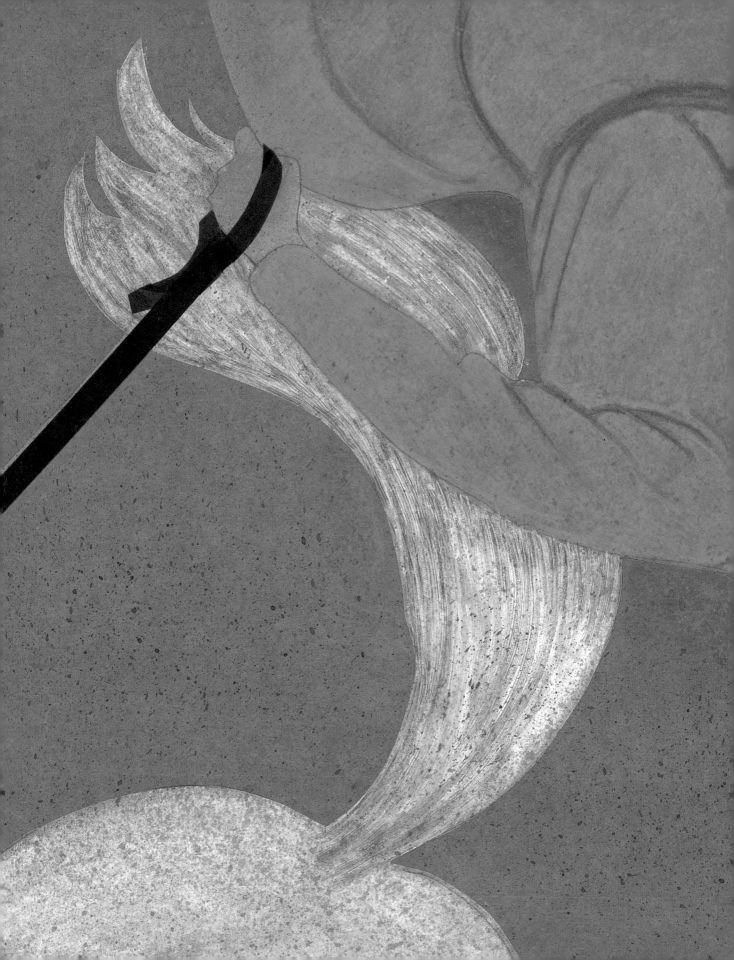

The next month Sai's son decided to take the mare for a ride. The horse threw him and he broke his leg.

When people came to console Sai, again he said,
"It could be this is not such a bad thing."

Later that year hostile nomads invaded China's northern border. All able-bodied men took up arms to defend their home.

Though peace followed, many did not return.
Because of his injury, Sai's son was spared.

Sai's son had learned from his father to trust in the ever changing fortunes of life. Together, for all the days that followed, Sai and his son lived in harmony.

Requests for permission to make copies of any part
of the work should be mailed to:
Permissions Department, Harcourt Brace & Company,
6277 Sea Harbor Drive, Orlando, Florida 32887-6777.

Silver Whistle is a trademark of
Harcourt Brace & Company.

Library of Congress Cataloging-in-Publication Data
Young, Ed.
The lost horse/Ed Young.
p.   cm.
"Silver Whistle."
Summary: A retelling of the tale about a Chinese
man who owned a marvelous horse and who
believed that things were not always as bad,
or as good, as they might seem.
ISBN 0-15-201016-5
[1. Folklore—China.]   I. Title.
PZ8.1.Y84Lp   1998
398.2'0951'02—dc21
[E]   96-52861

First edition
F E D C B A

The illustrations in this book were done in collage
with pastel and watercolor.
The text type was set in Bembo.
The display type was set in Serlio.
Color separations by Tien Wah Press, Singapore
Printed and bound by Tien Wah Press, Singapore
This book was printed on totally chlorine-free
Nymolla Matte Art paper.
Production supervision by Stanley Redfern
and Ginger Boyer
Designed by Michael Farmer

ABOUT THIS BOOK

In China the story of The Lost Horse is a proverb with four characters.
The Chinese calligraphy beginning this book narrates the original Chinese
story, and my English text is adapted from that in a fuller telling for readers
of all ages. There are also variations of "The Lost Horse" that exist
throughout the Middle East.

I first started the picture book telling of this tale more than twenty years
ago. Only recently did I realize that the story could be re-created in puppet
play, giving readers the chance to make it their own. I encourage readers to
extend the story beyond the limits of these pages.

ED YOUNG